Skateboarding

Carmel Reilly

Australia • Brazil • Japan • Korea • Mexico • Singapore • Spain • United Kingdom • United States

Skateboarding

Fast Forward
Yellow Level 7

Text: Carmel Reilly
Editor: Kate McGough
Designer: James Lowe
Series Design: James Lowe
Production Controller: Emma Hayes
Photo Research: Corrina Tauschke
Reprint: Siew Han Ong

Acknowledgements
The author and publisher would like to acknowledge permission to reproduce material from the following sources: Photographs by Age fotostock/ Brand X Pictures, p. 13/ SuperStock, p. 4; Alamy Images/ BananaStock, p. 8 top/ Buzz Pictures, p. 10/ Paul Gapper, p. 11 bottom/ Ingram Publishing, p. 8 bottom; Imagen/ Bill Thomas. p. 12; Lindsay Edwards. back cover, pp. 5 bottom, 14-16; Newsphotos.com/ Robert Pozo, pp. 3, 11 top/ Troy Snook, p. 9 bottom; Newspix.com, p. 5 top; Photo Edit/ Tony Freeman, p. 7/ Michael Newman, p. 6/ Photolibrary.com/ plainpicture, p. 9 top; Sport the library/ Steve Gourlay Skateboarding - Mute Tas Pappas - Action, cover, p. 1.

ISBN 978 0 17 012505 5
ISBN 978 0 17 012511 6 (set)

Cengage Learning Australia
Level 7, 80 Dorcas Street
South Melbourne, Victoria Australia 3205
Phone: 1300 790 853

Cengage Learning New Zealand
Unit 4B Rosedale Office Park
331 Rosedale Road, Albany, North Shore NZ 0632
Phone: 0800 449 725

For learning solutions, visit **cengage.com.au**

Printed in China by 1010 Printing International Ltd
7 8 9 10 11 18 17 16 15

THE UNIVERSITY OF MELBOURNE

Evaluated in independent research by staff from the Department of Language, Literacy and Arts Education at the University of Melbourne.

Skateboarding

Carmel Reilly

Contents

Chapter 1

SURFING ON THE STREET

Skateboarding has been around for over 40 years.

Surfers made the first skateboards. (Skateboards look like little surfboards.) They were made for surfers to ride when the waves were too flat to surf!

The first skateboards were made of wood. Now they are made of wood and other things.

Skateboarders do not need to go to special places to ride their boards.
They can ride them where it is hard and flat, like on the street or in car parks.

A lot of parks have made special places for skateboarding.
A lot of people go there to ride their boards
and to spend time with groups of skateboarders.

Chapter 2

THE COMMUNITY

Skateboarders are a part of a big group or **community**. This is called the skateboarding community. This is not a community of people who live in the same place. It is a community of people who like to do the same things.

People in the skateboarding community like to have special skateboarding clothes. They like to take their skateboards with them and ride them all the time!

Chapter 3

KEEPING FIT

Skateboarders have to work hard when they ride. They have to run, jump and swing around a lot.

Skateboarding is a good way for people to get fit, and to stay fit.

When they are very fit, skateboarders can move around and do a lot more on their boards.

Chapter 4

WORKING ON THE BOARD

Skateboarders do a lot of work on their boards to make them run well.

Skateboarders need their boards to be safe, so that they don't get hurt when they ride them.

They have to fix them
when they break.

Chapter 5

STAYING SAFE

Check that your skateboard is working well.

1. Check to see if the board or the wheels need to be fixed.

2. Check your hand and leg pads.

3. Check that your helmet fits well.

4. Ride your skateboard in a safe place, and tell people where you are going.

Glossary

community a group of people sharing the same interests

Index